Who's That I Hear?

Story by DJ Hill

Illustrations by Julie Adriansen

Editor, Jenniey Tallman

Published in the USA by Lucky Chicken Productions, LLC.

ISBN: 978-1-7327909-2-6

Library of Congress Control Number: 2020908250

**Visit OwletsCo.com
for activities, storytime,
and interactive games!**

Light of the Moon, Inc.
Partnering with self-published authors since 2009
Book Design/Production/Consulting
Carbondale, Colorado • www.lightofthemooninc.com

For Natalie, Liam, Finley, Tegan, Silas, Addison,
Carson, Kalyssa, Skylar, and children everywhere.

*"The more
that you read,
the more things
you will know.
The more that you
learn,
the more places you'll go."*

-Dr. Seuss

Bump, scritch, scratch

What's that noise? I heard a sound.
Now I'm looking all around.
Something's there, I just can't see.
Please oh please, oh don't eat me!

"Mom, help,
I need you.
Please come quick!"

I'm telling you I heard a sound …
not way up high, but on the ground.

"Go back to sleep.
It's just the wind."

Bump, scritch, scratch

There it is, that sound again.
A creature moving.
Not the wind.
I do not think I want to see
the great big monster after me.

"Help, I'm scared.
Mom, Dad: Come quick!"

"Look darling dear, there's nothing here.
The old floor creaks
so have no fear.
Your imagination's tricking you.
Now back to sleep, that's what to do."

Squeak. Peep. Squeak.
The pitter pat of little feet.

There's just one thing we need to do:
Listen closely.
Follow clues.

Be brave and hunt for monsters there …
or maybe it might be a bear.

It's getting louder, louder now.
Tiny squeaks, not great big growls.

I see it. Wait. That's no nightmare.
There are no monsters anywhere.

A tiny mouse and family …
who need a home just like me.

A place to be safe, cared for, and warm …
with people who love you and keep you from harm.

Good night little mouse
and your family.

Thanks for sharing
my room with me.

Julie Adriansen is a watercolorist living in Washington State. Her style of painting is simple. She embraces color and simple bold images. A lover of people and animals, she portrays her subjects using the colors she sees in them—hoping these are the same colors they see in themselves. Her goal is that her art stirs up the same feelings in her audience that she feels as she paints her subjects.

Community is important to Julie. She believes bringing people together through art makes the place we live better and more fulfilling. Art is something to be shared—it gives us the opportunity to experience beauty, emotion, expression, and joy.

Julie hopes you enjoy her work.

julieadriansenart.com

DJ Hill is a poet and mixed media artist. She lives and creates in Santa Fe, New Mexico. *Who's That I Hear?* is her first children's book.

Homespun Mercies, DJ's debut collection of poetry, won the NYC Big Book, IBPA Benjamin Franklin, and CIPA EVVY Awards in Poetry. It has also received honors from the Nautilus, IPPY, and International Book Awards.

Her mixed media art has been exhibited at the R2 Gallery, Red Brick Center for the Arts, Las Laguna Gallery, and Loveland Museum—where it was awarded the Spirit of the Suffragists prize during VOTE: A Centennial Celebration.

djhill-writer.com